First At Last
AND OTHER STORIES

JULIA McCLELLAND
Illustrated by
ANN JAMES

Oxford
Oxford University Press

OXFORD UNIVERSITY PRESS

Oxford New York Toronto
Delhi Bombay Calcutta Madras Karachi
Petaling Jaya Singapore Hong Kong Tokyo
Nairobi Dar es Salaam Cape Town
Melbourne Auckland
and associated companies in
Berlin Ibadan

OXFORD is a trade mark of Oxford University Press

© Text Julia McClelland 1991
© Illustrations Ann James 1991
First published 1991

A CIP catalogue for this book is available from the British Library

ISBN 019 553322 4

Published by Oxford University Press
Walton Street, Oxford OX2 6DP

First At Last

AND OTHER STORIES

First at
Last

Contents

For my family
and for Joan

for Boris

First At Last

Zachariah hated his name. It was too long, it sounded funny and, worst of all, it was always the last one on the list.

Amy, Ben and Catherine were at the beginning. Lance, Melanie and Nicholas were in the middle. Xavier, Yolanda and Zachariah were at the end.

The other kids teased him. They called out to him in the playground, 'Zachariah, Zachariah, we don't trust you — you're a liar!'

They were also mean to Xavier and Yolanda. They chanted, 'Xavier, Xavier, on your best behaviour!', and 'Yolanda, Yolanda, you look like a gander!'

The three victims would link arms, poke out their tongues and yell back, 'You're just stupid, you're just tame; you're just jealous of our names!'

1

Zachariah blamed his mother for his name, but she said, 'You have a very special name. It means "God has remembered him".'

'Well, he must have forgotten me pretty quickly,' grumbled Zachariah, 'because I'm always last.'

Then one Monday morning a new teacher arrived. She wrote her name on the blackboard: 'Miss Trams'. Some kids giggled and other kids snickered behind their hands.

Miss Trams said, 'I used to think Trams was a silly name too, until I looked at it backwards. Then I realized I was a very clever lady.' The children laughed and started calling her Miss Smart.

Two weeks later Miss Trams announced, 'I have a surprise for you. Today is going to be Backwards Day. We are going to look at the world differently for just one day.'

They began by trying to talk backwards. 'Zachariah, today you are how?' asked Miss Trams. Zachariah had to think for a long time before he slowly answered, 'Trams Miss you thank, well very am I.' Then Sarah very quickly asked, 'Trams Miss, excused be please I may?' before she rushed out.

At recess they put their jumpers on back-to-front and walked backwards. Gerard and Patrice crashed into each other and were very cross. 'We can't see where we're going!' they complained to their teacher. But Miss Trams just smiled and said, 'Precisely!'

They all enjoyed eating their lunch backwards. 'No one is allowed to touch their sandwiches until they've eaten all their cake and fruit first,' said Miss Trams.

During the afternoon they counted backwards from one hundred to one. They played 'Ladders and Snakes' by going up the snakes and down the ladders. They turned their desks around and faced the back of the room.

Gerard and Patrice crashed into each other and were very cross.

When they had to say the alphabet backwards, Zachariah was delighted.

'We all know the first letter,' said Miss Trams. 'It's Z for Zachariah.' After they had finally made it to A, Miss Trams called Zachariah out to the front. 'I know exactly what it's like to be always last on the list,' she told him. Then she bent down and whispered in his ear. Zachariah smiled a big smile.

He went back to his desk. His best friend, Rebecca, nudged him with her elbow. 'What's the big secret?' she whispered.

Very quietly Zachariah said, 'Don't tell anyone, but her first name is Zelda.'

Just before home time, Miss Trams clapped her hands for silence. 'Everyone, Day Backwards wonderful a for you thank. And now I'm going to speak forwards again.'

She began handing out a piece of paper to each of them. 'Please look carefully at our new class list,' she said. 'This is the way it will stay for the rest of the term.' And she winked at Zachariah.

Zachariah stared hard at the list of names. Nicholas, Melanie and Lance were still in the middle, but Amy was actually last for once. He stared for a bit longer, just to make sure.

Then Zachariah stood up, turned to the back of the room and yelled 'RAYHOO!' because he was first at last.

4

The Pet Party

Rebecca had decided to have a pet party for her eighth birthday. She invited every person in her class at school and told them that if they didn't have a pet they could wear fancy dress instead.

Zachariah wasn't happy about this. For a long time now he had constantly pestered his parents for a pet. He must have told them about five thousand times that what he wanted was a real live wombat called Wanda. But as yet nothing had turned up, so he would have to wear fancy dress to Becky's party. He wondered if he would be the only one there without a pet.

On the morning of the pet party, Zachariah lay in bed playing with two of his cuddly friends. One was Bruce, his tartan teddy, and the other was Wanda, his small wombat. He was so intent on his game that he did not notice his father coming in.

Zachariah's dad pounced on the animals, saying, 'Morning, everyone. How's Bruce Bear today? Looking pretty spruce, aren't you, Bruce?' Zachariah giggled, waiting for the next bit. His dad put Bruce back before he held the wombat high above his head.

'Watch out, all you monsters and baddies, because this is the one and only Wanda the Wonder Wombat!' He made her fly up to the ceiling and then down to where Zachariah and Bruce were waiting to welcome her.

After both toys had been settled under the blankets, Zachariah scrambled out of bed and raced past his dad. He ran into his parents' room and hugged his mother, who was still in bed. 'How are you feeling, Mum?' he asked.

'We're both feeling fine, thanks,' smiled his mother, patting her tummy. 'We just need a bit of a rest, that's all.'

'It's a pity the baby isn't born yet,' said Zachariah. 'It won't be able to see me dressed up for Becky's party.'

Zachariah's dad appeared in the doorway, holding a cup of tea for his wife. 'Never mind, sport,' he said. 'I'll be here to see you. Let's go and get it all ready while Mum has her cuppa. Then you can help me organize breakfast.'

At one o'clock, Zachariah was finally allowed to put on his costume. He pulled on some brown track-suit pants and a brown T-shirt with a picture of a wombat on it. For his feet there were brown furry slippers.

He looked at his homemade mask and cardboard ears and hoped that they looked a bit like a wombat. The last thing he had to put on was a cloak which his mother had made out of

He made her fly up to the ceiling.

an old blue table-cloth. On the back was a huge letter 'W' painted in bright yellow.

When he was ready, he stretched out his arms straight ahead of him and ran to the lounge to show his parents. He zoomed once around the room before his dad scooped him up and stood him on a chair.

'Look! Up on the chair! Is it a bird? Is it a plane?'

Zachariah's mother answered, 'No, it's Wanda the Wonder Wombat!'

Zachariah got down from the chair and took off his mask. He was feeling a bit sulky. 'I'd still rather have a *real* wombat than pretend to be one,' he grumbled.

His parents looked at each other. His dad patted the spare seat on the couch and said, 'Come over here, Wonder Zach. We've got some good news for you.' He nudged his wife. 'You tell him, Tess.'

As Zachariah sat down, his mother put her arm around him and said, 'When you get home from the party, there'll be a surprise waiting for you. Your dad's going out soon and he'll bring it back with him.'

Zachariah immediately began bouncing up and down on the seat, yelling 'Oh boy, oh boy! I can't wait!' Then he stopped long enough to ask, 'What is it? Is it a pet? A wombat? It is, isn't it?'

But his dad only winked at him and said, 'I guess you'll just have to wait and see, kiddo. By the way, bring the Birthday Girl with you — I think she'll want to see your surprise.'

Zachariah jumped up. 'Can I go over and tell Becky now? She asked me to get there before the other kids.'

'Well, it won't take you long to walk all the way next door,' said his mum. 'But I think you're forgetting something.'

'What?'

'The birthday present.'

'Whoops, sorry.' He picked up a parcel from the coffee table and kissed his mum. She straightened his cardboard ears.

'Now don't forget to say thank you to Becky's mother and be careful not to trip on your cape,' she said.

'Have a good time, WW,' said his dad, 'and don't fly too high or you might crash into a jumbo jet.'

Because it was a special occasion, Zachariah didn't leap over his back fence and turn up at Rebecca's back door as he usually did. He walked through the front gate and Rebecca met him at the front door.

She was wearing a witch's costume which included a horrible mask. A pointed witch's hat perched on her long red hair. She yanked off her mask and grinned, waving her broomstick at him. Her black cat wove around her legs, its tail in the air.

Zachariah was so put out that he forgot to wish his friend a happy birthday. Instead he said, 'Hey! That's not fair! You said to bring a pet *or* wear fancy dress — how come you get to have your cat *and* be a witch as well?'

'Because it's my birthday and I can do whatever I want!' said Rebecca. She was trying not to look at the present Zachariah was carrying. 'Anyhow, I'll bet you get a pet of your own pretty soon.'

Zachariah cheered up instantly. 'That's what I was going to tell you,' he said. 'My dad's going out and when he comes home he's bringing me a surprise — and I'm *sure* it's a pet wombat.' Then he remembered to add, 'And I want you to come with me to see it.'

Rebecca's mother came to the door and said, 'Hi, Zach, you look wonderful. Why don't you both come in now until the other children arrive?'

Once inside, Zachariah finally got around to giving Rebecca the present. She ripped off the wrapping paper and found a small Paddington Bear. He was wearing his hat and his blue duffle jacket and carrying his suitcase.

Rebecca's green eyes glowed as she cuddled the bear. 'Oh, Zach! He's lovely. I've always wanted my own Paddington.' Then she quickly hugged Zachariah, but he pushed her away saying, 'Okay, you've thanked me enough!'

10

She yanked off her mask and grinned.

The doorbell rang and Rebecca ran to welcome her guests, still clutching her Paddington Bear. Soon the rumpus-room was so full of children and pets that Rebecca's mum asked them all to go outside.

In the backyard there was a great deal of noise, as the dogs barked at the cats and the cats hissed and growled back. Patrice accidentally dropped her white mouse, which scurried into the kitchen and made Rebecca's mother scream. Gerard had very sensibly brought a strong container for his grass snake.

There were a few budgerigars in cages and Lance had a big white cockatoo which screeched 'Hello, cocky! Cocky want a cracker!' A pair of guinea-pigs seemed to be rather nervous when anyone came near them, while Melanie's tortoise quietly crawled under a bush and went to sleep.

Zachariah was pleased to find that he was not the only one in fancy dress. As they played party games he noticed a pirate, a princess, a ballet dancer, a Red Indian and a ghost. After he'd pinned the tail on the donkey, someone tapped him on the shoulder. He turned to find Batman and Robin peering at him through their masks.

'Hi, Wonder Wombat. Solved any crimes today?'

'Not yet, I'm afraid,' admitted Wonder Wombat.

The Caped Crusaders shook their heads sadly at him. 'Come on, Boy Wonder,' said Batman to his partner, 'it's time for us to go and save Gotham City.'

But Gotham City had to wait because just then Rebecca's mum called out, 'It's party time, everyone. Come and find a place to sit down.'

Two long trestle tables had been brought out onto the lawn while the children were playing. They were loaded with party food. In the centre of one was an enormous birthday cake shaped like a cat.

'Holy pet party!' yelled Robin. 'Look at that cat cake!'

The children pushed and jostled for a while but soon they settled down to eat, wearing animal party hats.

There were plates of party pies and sausage rolls and cocktail sausages with jugs of tomato sauce nearby. The chocolate crackles were very popular and so were the lamingtons and butterfly cakes, which disappeared quickly.

As sticky fingers grabbed for the last potato chips and slices of fairy bread, Rebecca's mum brought out trays of dessert. Everyone was given a little glass bowl full of red and green jelly. There was a big scoop of vanilla ice-cream to go with it and on top of the ice-cream there was a strawberry.

The animals were having their own party on another patch of lawn. Melanie's tortoise missed out because he slept through the whole thing.

Once 'Happy Birthday' had been sung and the eight candles had been blown out, the children began to leave. They collected their pets, pieces of birthday cake and little baskets of lollies. On their way out they said thank you to Rebecca and her mum.

Zachariah heard his name being called and saw his mother waving to him from over the fence. He knew what she wanted. He waved back and shouted, 'Okay, Mum, we're coming!' He grabbed Rebecca's arm. 'Come on, Becky. My wombat's nearly here. We have to hurry so we can beat Dad home. Quick!'

They rushed to the back fence, with Zachariah tripping on his cape and Rebecca tripping on her long witch's dress, but they managed to scramble over without tearing anything.

Once they were next door, they ran across the lawn just in time to see Zachariah's dad getting out of his car in the driveway. Pressed to the window was a dark, furry face and from its mouth lolled a length of pink tongue.

14

Pressed to the window was a dark, furry face.

Zachariah stopped dead at the sight. His mother crossed her fingers as his father opened the back door and picked up a moving bundle. He turned and offered it to his son, saying, 'What do you think of *this*, Wonder Boy?'

Zachariah was dumbfounded for a moment. Then he bellowed, 'Oh, Dad, a puppy! For me! It's beautiful! Oh, Mum, Becky — LOOK!' And he gave the puppy a big hug, and rubbed his cheek on the top of its head.

The creature squirmed and wriggled until it was in Zachariah's arms. Soon it was licking his face and neck and hands. Rebecca ran up to join in the cuddling and the puppy licked her as well. Then the children had to sit down as they realized there was really far too much puppy for them to hold.

Zachariah did not seem to mind at all that his pet was not a wombat. His parents smiled at each other and his mother said, 'He's wonderful, Donald, but isn't he rather large for such a young pup? I mean, he's half Zach's size already.'

Zachariah's dad brushed aside the question. 'Oh, I can't stand those namby-pamby little yapping things. This one will be a great friend for Zach when the baby comes and he'll guard the house, too.'

His wife asked, 'What sort is he, exactly?'

'Something called a Newfoundland, whatever that is,' said Zachariah's father offhandedly. 'Anyhow, don't worry, he probably won't get much bigger.'

Then they sat down with the children and shared the puppy — cuddles, licks and all. Zachariah's mother held the small face still for a moment, looked into the gentle eyes and said softly, 'I wonder if he'll want to call you Wanda . . .'

Sun, Sand And Sea

Zachariah did not call the puppy Wanda because he thought that would be silly. Instead he simply called him Wombat. Kids at school rolled their eyes and said, 'A dog called *Wom*bat?!' as though it was the most stupid thing they had ever heard. Only Rebecca seemed to understand.

'Don't forget I always wanted a horse. That's why I called my cat Pony,' she said. 'And it doesn't seem to matter so much any more because Pony's the best cat in the whole world.' As an afterthought she added, 'And she doesn't need as much room as a horse either.'

Zachariah thought his puppy was the best in the whole world too, but — unlike the cat called Pony — Wombat almost *did* seem to need as much room as a horse. Everyone in the family was convinced that he would never stop growing. Zachariah's dad loved to make jokes like: 'This must be the only dog who was grown up long before he was a grown-up.'

Zachariah had begged for the fast-growing puppy to be allowed to sleep on his bed. His parents finally gave in. What with Bruce the tartan teddy, Wanda the Wonder Wombat and a few other toy animal friends, the bed was becoming very crowded. Sometimes Zachariah wondered where *he* was going to fit. As the weather grew warmer, so did everyone in the bed. (Zachariah realized that Wombat would be wonderful in winter.) Still, no matter how hot they became, the two could not bear to be separated at night.

The school holidays finally arrived and Zachariah's family often went to the beach, which was a short drive from their house. Zachariah helped his dad pack the boot of the car with the big umbrella, a couple of folding chairs, the old picnic-basket, cold drinks, buckets and spades, flippers and snorkels, an inflatable beach ball, a tennis ball and a cricket bat.

Wombat helped Zachariah by bringing him any loose object he found lying around the garden, just in case it might be wanted. Zachariah's dad hastily shut the boot before Wombat could drop in an old chewed-up sneaker.

'Thanks, boy, but we won't need that today,' he explained to the prancing puppy. 'There'll be plenty of games for you to play at the beach.'

When Zachariah and Wombat were finally settled in the back seat, Zachariah's mum climbed slowly and heavily into the front. The baby was expected fairly soon but she insisted on going out with the others for the day. She laughed at her husband who fussed around adjusting her seatbelt: 'I *can* do it myself, you know.' Then she giggled as she received a huge slurpy kiss from one of the passengers behind her.

'Sorry, Mum,' said Zachariah, 'I'll swap places so he can't reach you. He can sit behind Dad instead.'

'Oh no you don't,' said his dad. 'I'm the driver around here — and that great furry lump is not going to lick *me*!'

18

She giggled as she received a huge slurpy kiss.

Wombat cheerfully turned his head from one to the other, panting twenty times a second and grinning because he knew they were talking about him. Just as Zachariah's dad was saying they really needed a bigger car, and Zachariah's mum was saying she really did not mind being kissed by a friendly dog, Wombat settled the matter. He sat quietly and stuck his head out the window, waiting for the engine to start.

'Anyhow,' said Zachariah, 'Macca will help me look after Mr Giant here.'

Macca's real name was Kevin McConnachie, but no one ever called him that. Even Mrs McConnachie was simply known as Macca's Mum. He lived a couple of streets away from Zachariah in a big old house with his five brothers and sisters. He didn't go to the same school as Zachariah, but the two of them often met at the local park to kick a football or to practise batting and bowling.

Soon they all piled out of the car at the beach. Wombat importantly carried the tennis ball in his mouth. Zachariah's mum was not allowed to carry anything except a beach-bag which contained enough sun-screen lotion and insect-repellent for everyone.

The boys threw down their towels, kicked off their thongs, smeared on sun-screen and yanked on their sun-hats. They were already wearing their bathers and T-shirts. Ready at last, they tore down to the water's edge to test the temperature with their toes. As one, they quickly leapt back again yelling, 'It's *freezing!*'

Wombat did not agree. He raced past them into the shallows, splashing madly and barking frantically at some seagulls. The gulls did not seem to be frightened — they just flapped lazily a little further out before settling down again on the calm surface.

Zachariah laughed and turned to wave at his mother, who was comfortably seated under the umbrella reading the newspaper. It was still quite early in the season and there

weren't many others on the beach. Zachariah's dad was carefully putting lotion on his feet because that was where most people always forgot to put it. Then he grabbed the bat and ball and strolled down to join the boys.

Wombat saw him coming and bounded out of the water to make sure he wouldn't be left out. Full of excitement, he leapt and yelped around the small cricket team until they all felt dizzy just from watching him. He ended the performance by giving his sopping shaggy coat one tremendous shake, sending sparkling drops of sea-water everywhere.

'Good grief!' said Zachariah's dad. 'I think we should make this chap our star fielder, don't you? He's got enough energy to chase a ball for miles.'

The boys got down to the serious business of considering which team they wanted to be — Australia, England or the West Indies. Or, as Macca put it, 'The Aussies, Poms or the Windies.'

They finally decided it did not really matter who they were, and the game began. They had been playing for some time when Zachariah's dad hit a six out to sea. 'Go, Wombat!' he shouted.

Wombat obediently splashed after the ball and retrieved it. Instead of dropping it at the bowler's feet, however, he made it clear that he wanted to play another game. With the ball firmly clamped between his teeth he bolted off along the beach. He didn't even wait to make sure he was being chased.

The boys yelled in surprise and were about to set off after him when Zachariah's dad stopped them. 'Hold on, team,' he said. 'My tummy tells me it's time to eat, even if the umpire disagrees. Leave that mutt alone and he'll soon be back.'

He was right. As soon as the team retired for lunch, the puppy realized that no one else wanted to play so he came careering back again, spraying water and sand along the way.

22

He gave his sopping shaggy coat one tremendous shake.

Everyone helped lay out the picnic on a big checked rug. Zachariah made sure Wombat had his own meal and water a short distance away. Macca's eyes darted eagerly from the picnic-basket to the rug and back again, as one wonderful item of food after another appeared. 'Wow! Get a load of this lot!' he shouted, trying not to grab everything at once.

To begin with there was cold chicken, ham quiche, salmon sandwiches, plenty of salad, and buttered brown bread rolls. After that there was strawberry tart and chocolate cake, washed down with cold lemonade or orange juice. They finished off with chunks of watermelon and pineapple, and Zachariah's parents had a cup of tea from the thermos. Wombat cheerfully ate up any scraps, not that there were many left to give him.

24

Zachariah's mum dug down deep into the bottom of the basket and brought out a few small chocolate bars and a couple of bananas. 'Anyone interested in these?' she asked. Although it was obvious that the chocolate bars had begun to melt in the heat, the boys still took them and began munching happily.

Zachariah's dad took the bananas, but instead of eating them he put one in each ear. Zachariah laughed delightedly when he saw this because he knew the routine. So did his mother. Macca, however, did not know what was going on. He nudged his friend.

'Why's your dad stuck bananas in his ears?' he asked through a mouthful of chocolate.

Zachariah's mum said, 'Why don't you ask him yourself?'

'Okay. Um, excuse me for asking this Mr Scott, but why have you got bananas in your ears?'

Zachariah's dad leaned forward a bit and the bananas leaned with him. 'What's that, laddie? I can't hear you.'

Macca stood right in front of him and shouted, 'I want to know why you've got bananas in your ears!'

Zachariah's dad shook his head and said, 'Sorry, mate, I can't hear you. I've got bananas in my ears.'

Macca laughed with the others and Zachariah explained, 'Dad's been doing that one for years — it's my favourite joke.'

Zachariah's dad was just suggesting that the boys wait an hour before going for a swim ('or you might get cramp') when Zachariah's mum suddenly made a strange noise. A little while later she made another one.

'What's up, Mum?' asked Zachariah. 'Have you eaten too much?'

His mother grabbed her husband's hand excitedly. 'This is it, darling!' she said. Zachariah stared at them.

'This is *what*, Mum? What's the matter?' he asked.

His dad grinned and said, 'Looks like we'd better pack up, men — and pronto.' He began tossing cups and plates willy-nilly into the basket, making his wife laugh and then clutch her stomach.

Zachariah thought his parents must be going round the bend. He put his hands on his hips and demanded, 'Mum, what's going *on*?'

'It's okay, Zach. Something wonderful's going on.' She smiled and put out her arms for a hug. 'The baby is on its way.'

Big Brother

Zachariah was lying in a strange bed, staring into the darkness. He knew he couldn't sleep, so he went over all the things that had happened since the picnic-lunch at the beach.

The plan had been simple. He was to stay at Macca's house because his dad would be at the hospital until the baby was born. He and Macca would have a great time playing footy or computer games or doing whatever they wanted. It had all sounded like it would be lots of fun.

Unfortunately, Wombat was not allowed to stay at Macca's house because there was not enough room for him. 'It's a big house, all right,' said Macca's mum, 'but when there are six children in it plus Zach, it's not *that* big.' So Zachariah's dad had taken Wombat home after dropping the boys at Macca's place.

Zachariah turned over in the narrow bed and squeezed his eyes shut tightly. He did not want to think about Wombat, who would not understand why they were separated. He also knew it was best not to think about Bruce the tartan teddy or Wanda the Wonder Wombat. He felt very lonely in bed without his familiar friends, but it was better than Macca making fun of him.

Macca did not take any soft toys to bed with him — he said they were only for babies. Zachariah didn't consider himself a baby, but then he had to admit he did not really know what babies were like. Macca, on the other hand, was an expert because he had younger brothers and sisters.

Zachariah thought about all those brothers and sisters. He remembered how he'd felt when the whole family had sat around the big dining-table for tea that evening. He was totally amazed by all the noise going on around him. While Macca's mum dished up roast lamb and vegetables and gravy, everyone seemed to talk at once. No one listened to anyone else and no one noticed that no one else was listening. They didn't seem to care.

Then suddenly there was silence when Macca's dad thumped the table and announced, 'All right kids, that's enough. Eat up now.' The children ate quickly and without speaking, except for the occasional complaint about the food. Mary hated pumpkin and Michael hated beans. They did a swap and were happy again. The entire family laughed when baby Kathleen bounced up and down in her high-chair, making the spoonful of mashed vegetable go down her front instead of into her mouth.

The noise level was even worse than before when the oldest girl and boy brought in the dessert. It was a huge apple pie with lots of plump sultanas and a sprinkling of cinnamon. There was a large jug of custard to go with it and also a bowl of thick cream. Someone demanded, 'Me first this time, Mum — it's my turn!' Someone else whined, 'Oh no, not custard with it — I'll *die* if I have to eat custard.'

Mary said she liked apricot better than apple; Michael said that he would eat hers if she was going to be fussy; Macca asked loudly for a big piece because he was a growing boy; the baby gurgled and squealed just for the fun of it; Macca's dad said, 'You're a great cook, Maggie'; and Zachariah said nothing, feeling stunned.

Now he lay quietly, thinking how different everything was in a large family. He missed his mum and dad and Wombat and he wanted to go home. He was trying hard not to cry when he heard someone talking downstairs and then footsteps coming up the stairs. A head poked around his door and a well-known voice said softly, 'You awake, Tiger?'

Zachariah leapt out of bed yelling, 'Dad! I missed you! Can we go to see the baby now?' He was picked up and swung in the air and hugged and tickled — and then swung and hugged again.

His dad was smiling all over his face. 'It's a little girl, Zach,' he said. 'You've got an absolutely beautiful, brand new baby sister.'

Zachariah bellowed, 'Oh — WOW!' and rushed over to Macca, who was sitting up groggily in the other bed, rubbing his eyes. 'Hey, Macca, guess what?'

Macca groaned, 'What time is it? What's going on?'

Zachariah jumped on the bed, climbed all over his friend, gave him a few friendly whacks on the shoulder and shouted, 'I'm a *big brother*!'

He was picked up and swung in the air.

Thirty seconds later, Zachariah had pulled on a track-suit over his pyjamas and was stampeding downstairs just ahead of his father. He stopped so suddenly on the bottom step that his father nearly flattened him. 'Zach, what on earth's the matter with you? You gave me a fright stopping like that.'

'Sorry,' said his son, 'but I just thought of something. It's about the baby. Please, Dad, whatever you do — don't call her Zelda!'

Away In A Manger

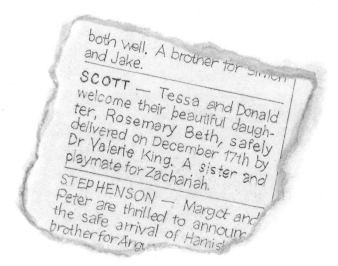

both well. A brother for Simon and Jake.

SCOTT — Tessa and Donald welcome their beautiful daugh-ter, Rosemary Beth, safely delivered on December 17th by Dr Valerie King. A sister and playmate for Zachariah.

STEPHENSON — Margot and Peter are thrilled to announce the safe arrival of Hamish, brother for Angus.

A week later it was Christmas Eve. Zachariah and Macca were at the local adventure playground. It was really too hot to do more than swing on the swings or slide down the slide. After a while they gave up and sat under a tree, attacking their little plastic bottles of frozen orange juice. Wombat helped himself to the puddle at the bottom of a leaking bubble-tap and then flopped down, panting loudly.

Zachariah grubbed around in his pocket and brought out a crumpled scrap of paper. He carefully smoothed it out and showed it to Macca. 'Oh, for Pete's sake,' said his friend, 'I've already seen it about five million times.'

Zachariah did not seem to mind. Holding up the scrap, he slowly and proudly read, 'SCOTT. Tessa and Donald welcome their beautiful daughter, Rosemary Beth, safely delivered on December 17th by Dr Valerie King. A sister and playmate for Zachariah.' He added, 'That's me, you know — that last bit.'

Macca shoved him. 'I *know* it's you, you great twit!' he laughed. 'Who else would it be?'

'I wish I could have brought Rosie along with us,' mused Zachariah. 'Maybe I could have pushed her on the swings.'

Macca stared at his friend and shook his head in disbelief. 'You really haven't got a clue, have you, mate? About babies, I mean.'

Zachariah shifted uncomfortably and crunched a mouthful of icy drink. 'Well, she's really cute, Macca — and it does say she's my playmate. I've never been a big brother before. I'll need lots of practice.'

'Listen, I know *every*thing about babies,' said his friend. 'They can be little monsters sometimes. I mean, they're always crying and they wreck all your toys and stuff.'

He looked at Zachariah's face and said, 'Oh well. I guess it's not that bad when you've only got one. I just wish there wasn't *always* a baby at our place . . .' His voice trailed away.

Zachariah jumped up and Wombat immediately stood next to him. 'Come on, let's go. It's too hot to play here. We'll collect Becky and find something else to do. We won't think about babies for a while, okay?'

They found that Becky was already at Zachariah's house, hanging over the baby's bassinet. She looked up happily as the boys tiptoed in. 'It's okay — she's awake,' she said. 'I'm looking after her while your mum's making a cup of tea.'

Macca turned to Zachariah. 'I thought we were going to forget about babies for a while,' he said. Zachariah shrugged his shoulders.

The three of them peered down at the tiny girl, who was waving her hands about. 'Watch this!' said Zachariah importantly, and he put his finger into one of the moving hands. Instantly, all the miniature fingers curled around the one big one and clutched it tightly. 'See that grip? She'll soon

The three of them peered down at the tiny girl.

be swinging on the monkey-bars, I reckon.' Carefully he uncurled the fingers again.

Macca looked at the fuzz of blonde hair and then at the cloudy blue eyes which tried to focus on him before they suddenly closed. He put his hand down and gently stroked the smooth little cheek. 'Hullo, Zach's kid sister,' he said softly. 'Your big brother was right — you *are* cute.'

'Told you,' said Big Brother smugly.

They heard a call from the kitchen. 'Anyone want a cuppa? Or a cold drink?' They trooped out for their snack, which offered more interest than a sleeping baby. As they sat around the kitchen table munching shortbread and mince pies with their drinks, Zachariah's mum said, 'I'm afraid this household has been a bit slack about Christmas this year. It's lucky your grandma brought over so many Christmas goodies for us to eat, Zach.'

'I'll say! Will she be bringing a pudding for Christmas dinner tomorrow?' asked Zachariah.

'Don't worry. She's promised. Anyhow, I was going to suggest that you three put up the tree and decorate it this afternoon,' his mother went on. 'I know it's nearly too late, but at least it will be ready for our visitors this evening.'

'Hey, yeah — that'd be great!' chorused the children.

'My mum and dad are really looking forward to coming,' said Rebecca.

'Yeah, so are mine,' said Macca.

'So is Wombat,' said Zachariah and they all laughed.

The children had a wonderful afternoon decorating the tree. When Zachariah had put the big golden star at the top, they all stood back and admired their work. Zachariah's mum came to join them.

Zachariah had put the big golden star at the top.

'What a talented team!' she said. 'It looks fantastic. And you've finished just in time, too. I think I heard the car, Zach.'

With Rebecca and Macca following, Zachariah rushed outside to meet his father. Wombat had beaten him to it. Zachariah's dad was backed up against the car, pretending to be frightened. 'Help! Somebody! I'm being attacked by a vicious monster!' He held up his hands to protect his face while Wombat leapt around him, barking and licking in a frenzy of welcome.

'Don't worry, Dad — I'll save you!' called Zachariah. He hurled his arms around Wombat's neck and then rolled onto the ground with the dog nearly squashing him. The other children flung themselves down to join in the wrestling game, but it was too hot to keep it going for long. Soon they were all up and romping around in the shade.

As Zachariah's dad kissed his wife, Wombat suddenly turned on an official warning bark and ran to the gate with the children in tow. Macca's parents and Rebecca's parents stood together uncertainly out on the footpath. They were clutching bottles and large cake tins.

'Hi, kids,' said Macca's dad. 'Is it safe to come in or are we likely to get eaten alive by that monster?'

Macca opened the gate but Rebecca pushed past him and hugged each of her parents. 'It's okay — I'll protect you all from the giant,' she giggled.

Nobody seemed to mind when the giant followed them all into the house. As soon as he reached the lounge-room, Wombat lay down exhausted at the foot of the Christmas tree and dozed off with his head on his paws.

Macca could not keep his eyes off the large dining-table, which was piled high with delicious things to eat. Zachariah's mum smiled at him and said, 'Come on, everyone. Help yourselves to whatever you like.'

Macca could not keep his eyes off the large dining table.

The children tended to ignore the cold chicken and ham and salads. They made straight for their favourite Christmas foods. As well as mince pies and shortbread, there were chocolate rum-balls and slices of rich, dark fruit cake.

They cheerfully drank sparkling apple cider while their parents had champagne. Zachariah's dad raised his glass and said, 'To Rosie's first Christmas,' and everyone said the same thing and had another drink.

Even though it was not quite Christmas, they all pulled crackers and read out the silly jokes to one another. Then Macca's dad took the purple paper crown from his cracker and put it on the sleeping dog's head. Everybody laughed and Rebecca's dad took a photo.

40

When the children finally finished their feast, they were not just full of food — they were also worn out. Zachariah lowered himself to sit with his back propped up against Wombat's warm flank. There was plenty of room left, so Rebecca and Macca sat on either side of him.

Baby Rosemary was brought in and the six grown-ups gathered round her, saying, 'Oh, what a dear little thing,' and 'Isn't she a pet?' They were all talking at once but it didn't seem to matter. The three children were not talking at all. They gradually closed their eyes and felt Wombat breathing gently against their backs.

When Zachariah opened his eyes again some time later, he saw his mum sitting on the couch, slowly rocking the baby in her arms. While she rocked, she softly sang 'Away In A Manger'. The other mothers joined in. So did Zachariah's dad.

Zachariah wanted to sing too but he could not wake up properly. He heard the hall clock chime and he counted twelve strokes. Midnight at last.

He smiled at his tiny sister and said, 'Happy Christmas, Rosie.' Then he went back to sleep.